Princess Smartypants

Breaks the Rules!

To Zack

PUFFIN BOOKS
Published by the Penguin Group: London, New York, Australia,
Canada, India, Ireland, New Zealand and South Africa
Penguin Books Ltd, Registered Offices: 80 Strand, London WC2R 0RL, England

puffinbooks.com

First published 2009
1 3 5 7 9 10 8 6 4 2
Text and illustrations copyright © Babette Cole, 2009
Made and printed in China
Hardback ISBN: 978–0–141–38361–3
Paperback ISBN: 978–0–141–50155–0

Princess Smartypants

Breaks the Rules!

Babette Cole

PUFFIN

"Just look at you, Princess Smartypants," said her mother, the Queen. "You will never get a prince like that!

You are going to fairy princess finishing school to learn how to behave **properly!**"

Princess Smartypants went to see her father. "Must I really go, Daddy?"

"Your mother will give you a hard time if you don't," said Kingy.

"I'll have to give it a try then,"
    said Smartypants.

Her arrival at Madame Twinklebotham's
Academy for Fairy Princesses
caused quite a stir!

"I know a trouble-maker when I see one," scolded Madame Twinklebotham.

"LOOK AT MY GIRLS!
That wretched dragon spooked their coaches
and most of them ended up in the moat!
Your lessons start NOW . . ."

DAY 2: Deportment and Fashion Sense

DAY 3: Weaving and Spinning . . .

your golden tresses long enough . . .

DAY 4:
. . . so that princes
can climb up them.

"You are being deliberately disruptive, Smartypants!" growled Madame Twinklebotham. "That's one week's detention in the dungeons!"

So Princess Smartypants
called her next-door ogre,
Cyril Sledgehammer.

He soon got her out.

"We want to be a cool princess like you," said her classmates. "We are bored with being fairy princesses."

"OK," said Princess Smartypants. "LESSON 1 . . .

Stop waiting for a bunch
of Hooray Henrys to turn
up and save you!"

"LESSON 2: Learn to govern your own kingdom."

"LESSON 3: You're going to need some muscle sometime so get those beasties on your side!"

Just then, Madame Twinklebotham burst in!
"WHAT ARE YOU DOING NOW, SMARTYPANTS?"

"LESSON 4," continued
Princess Smartypants.
"Wands do a bit MORE
than just wave…"

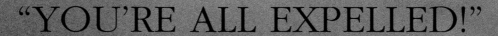

"YOU'RE ALL EXPELLED!"
squeaked the new Madame Twinklebotham.

"And most importantly . . ." laughed Princess Smartypants.
"LESSON 5: Let's break ALL the rules!"

So they all lived happily ever after!